SUPER SPORTS STORIES

PEDRO'S PERFECT PITCH

by Blake Hoena
illustrated by Christos Skaltsas

GRASSHOPPER

Tools for Parents & Teachers

Grasshopper Books enhance imagination and introduce the earliest readers to fiction with fun storylines and illustrations. The easy-to-read text supports early reading experiences with repetitive sentence patterns and sight words.

Before Reading

- Discuss the cover illustration. What do readers see?
- Look at the glossary together. Discuss the words.

Read the Book

- Read the book to the child, or have him or her read independently.
- "Walk" through the book and look at the illustrations. Who is the main character? What is happening in the story?

After Reading

- Prompt the child to think more. Ask: Why do you think Coach Ken thought Pedro would make a good pitcher? Was Coach Ken right? How do you know?

Grasshopper Books are published by Jump!
5357 Penn Avenue South
Minneapolis, MN 55419
www.jumplibrary.com

Library of Congress Cataloging-in-Publication Data

Names: Hoena, B. A., author. | Skaltsas, Christos, illustrator.
Title: Pedro's perfect pitch / by Blake Hoena; illustrated by Christos Skaltsas.
Description: Minneapolis, MN: Jump!, Inc., [2024]
Series: Super sports stories | Includes index.
Audience: Ages 7-10.
Identifiers: LCCN 2022048392 (print)
LCCN 2022048393 (ebook)
ISBN 9798885243919 (hardcover)
ISBN 9798885243926 (paperback)
ISBN 9798885243933 (ebook)
Subjects: CYAC: Baseball–Fiction. | Pitching (Baseball) – Fiction. | LCGFT: Sports fiction. | Readers (Publications)
Classification: LCC PZ7.H67127 Pe 2024 (print)
LCC PZ7.H67127 (ebook)
DDC [Fic] –dc23
LC record available at https://lccn.loc.gov/2022048392
LC ebook record available at https://lccn.loc.gov/2022048393

Editor: Eliza Leahy
Direction and Layout: Anna Peterson
Illustrator: Christos Skaltsas

Printed in the United States of America at Corporate Graphics in North Mankato, Minnesota.

Table of Contents

The Perfect Position

Pedro steps up to home plate. "You can do this," he mumbles, trying to calm himself.

It is the first day of practice with his team, the Cardinals. It is his first turn at bat.

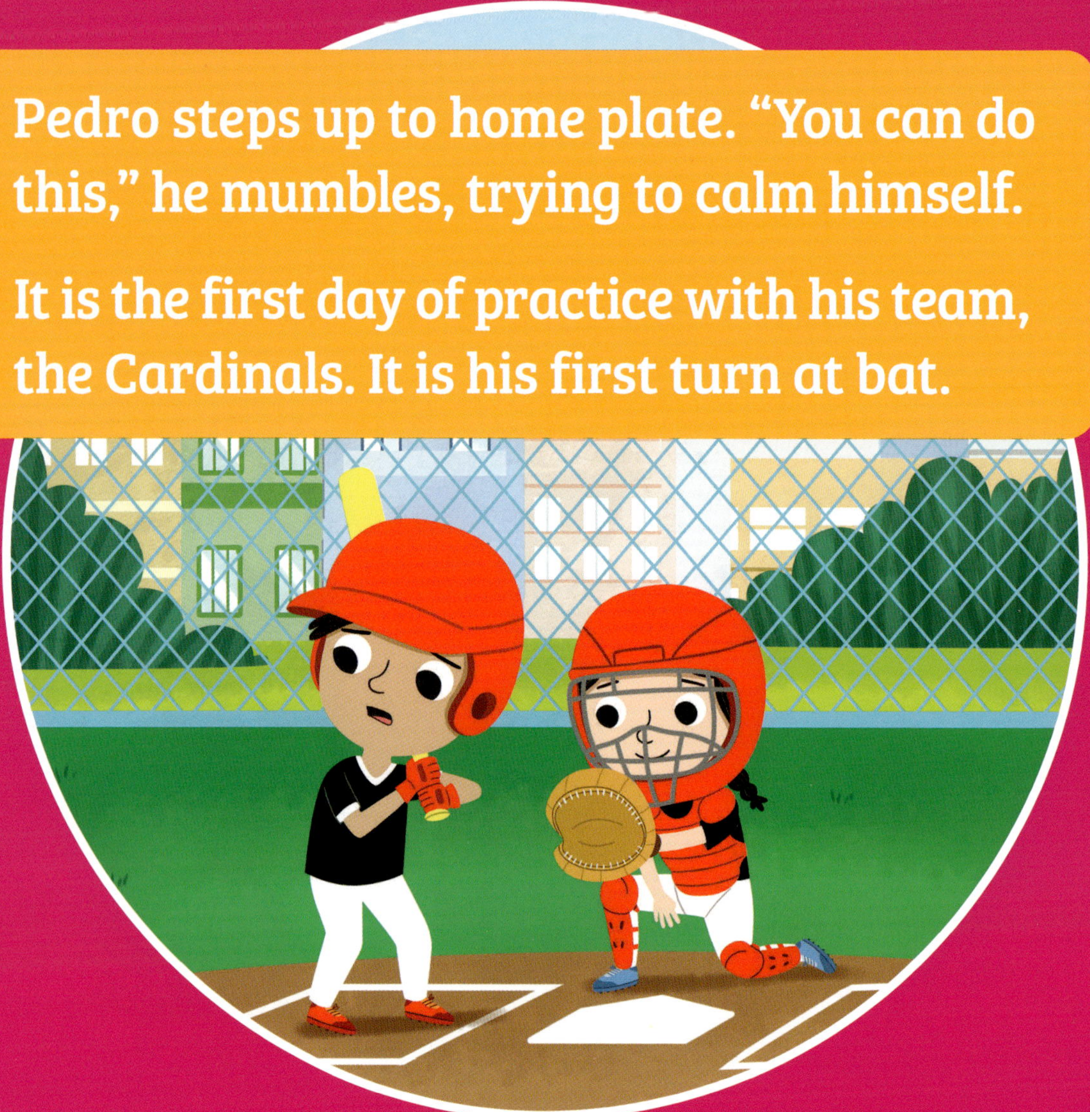

Coach Ken pitches the baseball.

Pedro swings the bat. *Crack!*

The ball sails over the third baseperson's glove and into the outfield.

"You're a natural hitter, Pedro!" Coach says. "But what position would you like to play in the field?"

"I'm not sure," Pedro says with a shrug. "I've never been on a team before. Could I try infield?"

"We need someone at second base," Coach says. "Let's put you there."

At second base, the first ball hit to Pedro is a line drive.

Pedro ducks and yells, "Ahhh!" as the ball zips by him.

"Hmm," Coach says. "Maybe we'll try you in the outfield instead."

Out in left field, the first ball hit to Pedro is a fly ball.

Pedro closes his eyes and says, "I hope I catch it! I hope I—"

Plop! The ball lands in the grass next to Pedro.

"Rats," he mumbles.

Pedro picks up the ball and throws it as hard as he can to Magdala at shortstop.

Smack! The ball hits Magdala's glove.

"Nice throw, Pedro!" Coach Ken says. "You have a great arm. Would you like to try pitching?"

"I practice throwing with my dad," Pedro says with a smile. "But I've never pitched before. I can try."

"Great!" Coach says. "Head over to the mound. You can practice."

Pedro's teammate, Ryan, steps up to the plate.

Pedro is nervous. *What if I'm not good at pitching?* he thinks.

Pedro takes a deep breath. Then he winds up and throws the ball toward Ryan.

Ryan swings. *Whoosh!* He misses!

"That was a perfect pitch, Pedro!" Coach Ken says. "I think we found your position in the field."

The next week, Pedro pitches for the Cardinals' first game. His team is up 5 to 4 as he faces the final batter.

Pedro winds up and pitches.

The batter swings and misses!

"Strike three!" the umpire yells. "Out!"

HOME
5
9
INN
GUEST
4
BALL
STRIKE
OUT
22

The Cardinals win!

Pedro's teammates cheer and gather around him.

"I did it. I did it!" Pedro shouts as his teammates high-five him.

Let's Review!

Pedro plays pitcher. What are the other baseball positions? Take a look!

1. **pitcher:** Stands on the pitcher's mound and pitches to batters.
2. **catcher:** Plays behind home plate and catches pitches from the pitcher.
3. **first baseperson:** Plays in the infield at first base.
4. **second baseperson:** Plays in the infield between first and second base.
5. **third baseperson:** Plays in the infield at third base.
6. **shortstop:** Plays in the infield between second and third base.
7. **left outfielder:** Plays in the outfield behind third base.
8. **center outfielder:** Plays in the outfield behind second base.
9. **right outfielder:** Plays in the outfield behind first base.

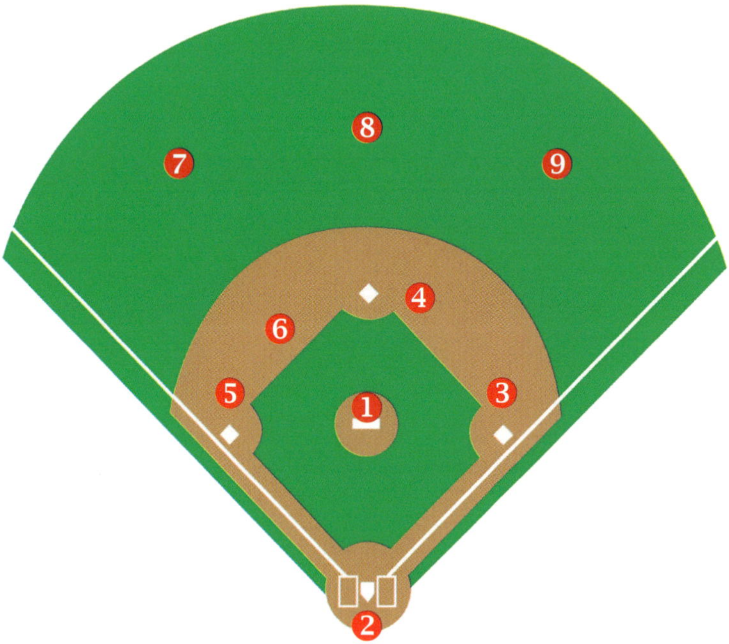

Baseball Equipment

What equipment does Pedro need to play baseball? Take a look!

To Learn More

Finding more information is as easy as 1, 2, 3.

1. Go to www.factsurfer.com
2. Enter "**Pedro'sperfectpitch**" into the search box.
3. Choose your book to see a list of websites.

Glossary

fly ball: A ball hit high in the air.

infield: The area of a baseball field where the four bases are found.

line drive: A ball that is hit hard and flies straight through the air.

mound: A raised area in the middle of the infield where the pitcher stands.

outfield: The grassy area of a baseball field beyond the bases.

position: A particular role on a team.

strike: A ball pitched over home plate between the batter's chest and knees or any pitch that is swung at and missed.

umpire: An official who calls plays during baseball games.

Index